1/21

ASTER'S
Map
of the
Valley

Forest

SNOW!
NOT TOO LAME

OLD LADY WITH DOGS???

NOTHING BUT GEEZERS

Translation copyright © 2020 by Dupuis
Cover art and interior illustrations copyright © 2018, 2020 by Dupuis

Published in the United States by RH Graphic, an imprint of Random House Children's Books, a division of Penguin Random House LLC, New York. The titles in this work were originally published in two separate volumes in the French language in Belgium as *Aubépine 1: Le génie saligaud*, copyright © 2018 Dupuis by Thom Pico & Karensac, and *Aubépine 2: Le renard furax*, copyright © 2018 Dupuis by Thom Pico & Karensac, by Éditions Dupuis S.A., Marcinelle, in 2018. All rights reserved.

RH Graphic with the book design is a trademark of Penguin Random House LLC.

Visit us on the Web! RHKidsGraphic.com • @RHKidsGraphic

Educators and librarians, for a variety of teaching tools, visit us at RHTeachersLibrarians.com

Library of Congress Cataloging-in-Publication Data
Names: Pico, Thom, author. | Karensac, illustrator. | Smith, Owen (Owen M.), translator. | Smith, Anne Collins, translator. | Pico, Thom. Génie saligaud. English. | Pico, Thom. Renard furax. English.
Title: Aster and the accidental magic / Thom Pico and Karensac ; translated by Anne and Owen Smith.
Description: First Random House Graphic edition. | New York : Random House Graphic, an imprint of Random House Children's Books, a division of Penguin Random House LLC, 2020. | "Originally published in two volumes, Aubépine 1: Le génie saligaud, and Aubépine 2: Le renard furax, in France by Dupuis in 2018." | Summary: Aster is bored at her new home in the mountains in the middle of nowhere—until she meets an odd old shepherdess and her woolly dogs, a sneaky trickster, and an angry fox.
Identifiers: LCCN 2019014042 (print) | LCCN 2019017516 (ebook) | ISBN 978-0-593-11886-3 (ebook) | ISBN 978-0-593-12417-8 (hardcover) ISBN 978-0-593-11884-9 (trade) | ISBN 978-0-593-11885-6 (lib. bdg.)
Subjects: LCSH: Graphic novels. | CYAC: Graphic novels. | Country life—Fiction. | Dogs—Fiction. | Foxes—Fiction. | Genies—Fiction. | Magic—Fiction.
Classification: LCC PZ7.7.P523 (ebook) | LCC PZ7.7.P523 As 2020 (print) | DDC 741.5/944—dc23

Designed by Patrick Crotty
Translated by Anne and Owen Smith
Thanks to Gina and Anton

MANUFACTURED IN CHINA
10 9 8 7 6 5 4 3 2 1
First American Edition

A comic on every bookshelf.

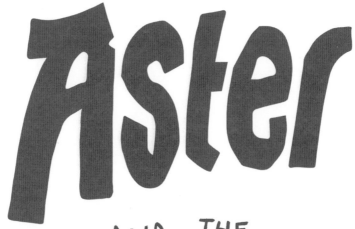

Aster

AND THE

ACCIDENTAL MAGIC

Story and Script
THOM PICO

Story and Art
KARENSAC

To Julien, Guillaume, Bola, Élisa,
Laurence, Stéphane, and Jonathan

MAKES SOME
POORLY THOUGHT-THROUGH WISHES

CLAK

Stupid Reed... him and his stories about monsters...I bet he just didn't want to get stuck here with me.

PLOP

CLICK

And don't forget, the great migration will occur next Saturday evening.

During this emergency, we advise all affected residents to evacuate to designated shelters or barricade yourselves indoors.

Fear is gripping the region, and even though the revolutionary Robo-Bird project is advancing quickly, the big question is—will it be ready in time?

We posed the question to the project director, Professor Rose...

Same old story! Migration here, migration there! It's getting ridiculous!

I can't believe people are getting so freaked out over a few birds.

ZAP

MOM?

Yes, sweetie?

The TV keeps talking about how the crows are gonna come and destroy everything...

Yes, I know, sweetie.

Did we really come here just because of this cruddy migration?

It's my job.

So, how are you going to stop them? Are you making a killer robot or what?

It's more complicated than that, sweetie.

Why not kill them? Aren't they mean?

Listen to me carefully, dear. It's not the birds' fault.

You shouldn't talk that way...they're not so old.

Okay, it's true that the village is deserted, but if all goes well, everyone will return in a few days!

Besides, there are some really interesting people around here. The shepherds, for example. When I was little, everyone kept praising them for protecting the mountain during the migrations.

And how will they defend themselves against giant angry birds? That's stupid.

Don't ask me—it's some sort of tradition.

Actually, it's a form of cultural atavism arising from the region's isolation. You know, like insular conduct.

What did she say?

Just smile and nod.

I will admit, it feels weird to be here. I haven't been back since our house was destroyed in the last migration. I wonder if the granny with the woolly dogs is still here.

Well, I doubt she's still alive. She was already as old as dirt when I was a kid!

It's not cool to make fun of fossils, Dad.

That night...

This place stinks!

What if that numbskull Reed was right?

Monsters would love to live in this house—it makes perfect sense!

What am I saying?! Monsters aren't real, it's all just make-believe!

Arrgh! I hate this place. Nothing ever happens here. It's so dead.

We're all alone here. No sounds, no light...

CLINK

Do you like the mountain?

Um...it's really pretty.

I think the mountain likes you too.

Really? Um... that's nice.

The mountain doesn't like just anybody. It won't even recognize some people whose families have lived here for generations. They'd never be able to find their way here—but you did.

But I got here by accident...

Hmm...by accident, you say? There are hidden corners on this mountain that few people can find—certainly not those who run away every time the birds migrate. Only those who are guided by the mountain.

I can tell you're not from around here, but you're no ordinary girl—you have the mountain inside you.

Uh, okaaay. Would you happen to be one of the old shepherds that my dad told me about? The ones who protect the valley, I mean?

By the wind's twelve quarters! No one's ever called me old before. Nowadays, there's no one left to protect the mountain but me.

Well, you don't have to worry—my mother is going to fix everything! She's an ornithologist, and she is too smart to foul up.

I see...you won't hold it against me if I stay on guard, will you?

Tell me, do you like my dogs? They're woolly!

Well...they are pretty cute.

I always say, there's nothing better for guarding a mountain than a woolly dog. I tell you what...take that little one there.

YIP!

He's very nice, but his coat won't grow. He'll never be any good for wool. But he'll make you a good companion.

YIP!

I'd love to, but I can't! My parents would never agree.

Parents only see what they want to see and only know what they want to know. You're lonely—I can tell. He'll be a good friend, and with him at your side, the mountain will always look after you.

Now take him and be on your way. You have far to travel if you wish to return home before nightfall.

But...

Er, well...thank you! See you later...

I hope so.

So, we're going to spend a lot of time together!

YIP!

The next day...

YIP!

Ouch! What happened?

You have walked in like a beauty.

Umm... who are YOU?

I am what humans would call a "trickster"!

O-kay. And what is your name?

MY NAME! You encounter a being of pure magic, born from the universal chaos at the beginning of the world and endowed with unbridled power, and your only desire is to know my name?

Well, yeah...

I'm not very interested in names.

Really? Well, I'm Aster, and I'm not very interested in strange toad-faced gasbags who refuse to give me their name!

It's just good manners!

Pffft, well, if you insist... I am the trickster

What?

I am the trickster Rapscallion!

I get wishes?

Of course! All trickster spirits are contractually obligated to grant wishes.

THREE WISHES*

*Standard rules and restrictions apply!

FIRST: No do-overs! You can't use one wish to cancel another wish.

SECOND: Keep your wishes out of my backyard!

No wishes can affect my clearing.

THIRD: Wait your turn! I serve only one client at a time.

Although nobody ever comes out here, so it's not usually a problem.

Wow! You have an awful lot of rules.

Well, I give awful service! Or is it awesome service? I forget. First wish, please! The end-user agreement requires immediate activation.

This is all a bit sudden...I'm just not sure...

It's not hard! What do you need right now?

Well...a friend to talk to.

How sad!

It'll be okay. I'm sure I'll learn a lot from you, Rapscallion!

YIP!

I want to be able to speak with Buzz!

Are you quite sure?

Yes!

I have no idea what just happened.

Well, it didn't meet the criteria for a hallucination.

Are you sure? It was too bizarre to be real.

Trust me, dreams about pit-dwelling magic tricksters who grant wishes are well beyond the capacity of most dogs. As a rule, we dream about dead squirrels.

I imagine so.

Wait...

YOU CAN TALK?!

Of course.

HOW BRILLIANT!

Really?

We'll be best friends and talk about all sorts of things—we'll have a great time together!

I thought we were best friends already.

You know, we can have good times together without talking.

True...but it's just not the same.

It's rather unusual for dogs to spend much time discussing matters. We prefer showing our feelings rather than talking about them. That's why dogs get along so much better than people.

Oh man! I can't believe it—a talking dog who's smart! Imagine the possibilities!

Reed is gonna be so jealous!

It's getting late...shouldn't we be heading home?

Holy cow! I can't believe it's night already! We'll have to hurry!

YIP!

yip!

ASTER!

Get back here!

Sit down, my pet. We need to talk.

Yip?

I know we told you we'd only be here for a short time. But things have changed.

?

My work is quite complex, so my project will require us to spend an entire year in the mountains. Your dad is going to find a local job soon.

At first, to get you used to the idea, we thought we'd tell you it was just temporary.

I must say how very proud we are that you have adapted to the area so quickly.

Dear, is something the matter?

Yip! Ruff ruff! Yap woof grrr? Yap arf arf!

(Of course something is the matter! How could you do this to me? You expect me to sit and stay like a...)

Just in time for dinner.

Blech! What's that smell? It reeks in here!

Ah—the odor—it's far stronger than yesterday. Even humans can smell it now...

SNIFF

Wait—why are there only two plates?

Woof?
(Hello?)

We should notify the rescue squad...

Good idea—oh no! The network is down again. How annoying!

She might get herself killed!

I know, honey...

But there's nothing we can do to help them.

YAAAAH

ROAR

KRIAA

POW

Oh my stars! What are you two doing here?!

ROAR

Yap! Grrr yap yap woof yip!

(Help us! We're trying to get everything back to normal!)

Yip!

By the wind's twelve quarters, child, I can't understand a word you're saying! Stand back—I have a mountain to protect.

Is she...?

Yes! I think so!

I'm the reason she's dead. If only I hadn't made those silly wishes...

If Mom had been here with her robot, none of this would have happened.

It's not Granny's fault. It's not even the birds' fault. I'm the one who's responsible...

I'm afraid we have no choice but to seek Rapscallion's help. If you phrase your last wish properly, perhaps he can set everything straight.

Sniffle

Let's go.

Well, well, well. Once again, the chosen one graces me with her presence. Has everything gone as you wished?

Stop making fun of me!

Me? Make fun of you? Never! All I did was give you exactly what you wished for.

You must have read stories about tricksters—we all behave the same way. It's not our fault humans never remember what they read.

Nothing turned out the way I wanted!

How was I supposed to guess what you wanted? I'm just a trickster—not Google.

But a person is dead!

FwHOOSH

CRACK

Tap Tap

Well, it's you! I haven't seen you in a dog's age! What brings you here?

Yip! Woof! Yip!

Oh—you want your second wish? What do you have in mind? Do you want to cause some trouble—or keep me from causing trouble?

ASTER+
BUZZ's
Map
of the
Valley

Forest

DANGER

GRANNY ♡

STILL
LAME

Aster

GETS A MAGICAL FOX
EXCEEDINGLY UPSET

Hmm...trouble's coming. I can sense it...

Hey, new kid! Wanna come play by the river with me and my buddies?

Thanks for asking, but I already have plans.

Suit yourself! Say, will your dog be waiting for you again today?

Of course—he can tell time.

Hey, don't try to con me...

Welcome home!

Is school over already? How about a video game?

Thanks, Dad, but I'd rather take a walk.

Again?! You're never home anymore—you're always outside!

You can't spare even a little time for your old dad?

ONE PLAYER

It's not you, Dad— when winter comes, it'll be too cold to go outside.

If you like, you can come along.

Nah. I grew up here—nothing ever happens.

It's just that with your mom and brother gone, there's not a whole lot to do around here.

Dad, are you planning to spend the whole day online?

It'll do you good to get outside for a change!

Don't forget, we're having pasta at eight!

I'm fed up with pasta!

Learn how to cook! Kissies!

Let's see...

"cookingforbeginners.com"

Yoo-hoo! Granny! Where are you?

Handling this summer's bird migration doesn't give you the right to call me Granny, child.

Yikes! Where did you come from?

Never you mind. What brings you out this way?

Nothing in particular... I just haven't seen you for a while.

It's not a good day for a visit.

Gently, dogs, gently!

Something's not quite right, and I don't want you underfoot if there's a problem.

Oh! Is there anything I can do? I'd like to help if I can.

It's kind of you to offer, but my troubles are my own. Even if, as you say, You managed to trick Rapscallion into bringing me back to life.

Why are you so worried?

It's autumn. Any moment now, autumn will arrive.

You know I'm very fond of her, Buzz, but she loves to make mountains out of molehills.

YIP!

Buzz, although I can't speak Dog anymore, you still seem to understand everything I say.

I sure could use your advice now, but there's no way I'm ever going back to that Rapscallion of a trickster spirit again!

We shall see...

Well, Dad, what have we here?

Whole pan-seared trout with broccoli and stewed squid!

Um...okay. But why?

Well, since you're at school all day, your mother's off in the wilderness somewhere studying birds, and your brother's away at college, I thought I might finally learn how to cook...

It's a great idea, Dad. But how about starting with something less, well, exotic?

You needn't be so quarrelsome. The Queen of Spring, after all, is always courteous.

If she wants to be all sweetness and light when you meet, that's her affair. I'm not interested in any small talk—just give me the crown!

Your feeble attempts to delay the inevitable infuriate me!

You become more ill-mannered every year... My time is over. The crown is yours!

At last!

CRRRK

What?

FFFFFFF

Heh, heh. Silent but deadly...

AAAAAOOOOOUUUUHH

AAAAOOOUUUUHH

AAAOOOOOUUUHHHH

ASTER!

For heaven's sake, Aster, wake up!

Just five more minutes, Buzz...

BUZZ?!

Did you just talk?

I'll explain later! Come on! It's an emergency!

Buzz?

Wait!

SCRR

BAM

What's going on, Buzz? You have to tell me!

It's Granny! She must be in mortal peril! The big dogs have been howling continuously for an hour!

Oh no! She's not dead again, is she?

I don't know, but I hope she's not going to make it a habit!

GRANNY!

She's still breathing! But she needs medical care—I'll call an ambulance right away!

BONK

Let's not get carried away. Help me get to my cabin. I have everything I need there.

B-b-but...

And stop stammering! You sound like a sheep—and I loathe those filthy beasts!

Click

Aster, let's head home. We're in the way here.

If the dogs don't need my help caring for her, why did they summon me?

Um...Does it matter? We prefer not to speak of it...even among ourselves.

I'm not in the mood for riddles.

Well, it's just...

While we dogs are very intelligent, we are occasionally vexed by...doors...

Doors?

Yes, doors. The concept is simple, and we understand them in theory, but we lack certain...appendages, you see.

Oh.

Well, when you put it that way, it makes perfect sense.

Really? You don't find it ridiculous?

Nah.

By the way, when were you going to tell me that you can speak Human?

I had acquired a taste for talking with you, and I missed our chats. So I devised a way to remedy the situation.

Don't tell me you did something stupid, like going to see the trickster Rapscallion!

Don't disparage my plan! I formulated my second wish precisely, and voilà! We can talk.

So why didn't you tell me sooner?

I was waiting for just the right moment. I know how sensitive you get whenever trickster spirits are mentioned.

You're not angry with me, are you? We're still friends?

TWIP.

Silly.

Ridiculous. It's completely ridiculous.

My reputation would be ruined if anyone saw those dogs chase me off.

Attention! No living being may watch what I'm about to do!

Ah—it's good to be king.

All right! If I must!

Dagnabbit...how do I get myself into these situations?

You know we can hear you, right? Would it hurt to show a little respect?

Silence!

I'm just sayin'...

Present arms!

The CHESTNUT KNIGHTS

HULL   LEAF   BURR

Okay, I'll make this simple: I've been outfoxed.

I don't know how, but that old crow has managed to divide the power of the Crown of Seasons.

I can't overstate the gravity of the situation...her all-too-human lust for power has put the entire valley at risk.

Oh dear! But what do you want us to do, boss?

Investigate. Survey the area. Find anything that could be useful to me.

By your command, boss!

Forward, Chestnut knights!

Uh... yeah...

I couldn't sleep, so I went out for a little walk.

Oh?

You need to be careful, Aster—it can be dangerous outside.

Chill out, Dad! Giant bird season is over!

Hmm...

SLURP

SLURP AH!

Okay, time for another walk.

Think again, young lady!

Wait, what?

It's a school day, isn't it?

Wait— isn't it Saturday?

"Nice try, Aster! I may not have a job, but I still know what day it is! And if I'm not mistaken, Friday is a school day!" Blah blah blah.

Argh! I was so sure it was the weekend!

Wait—it really is Saturday! ARGH! Bravo, Dad!

Way to go, Mr. "I Still Know What Day It Is!"

TAP TAP

SCREEEECH

So, whatcha doin' here, new kid?

It's silly, but I thought we had school today...

Of course there's no school today—we're on break, duh!

I guess when you skip school for weeks at a time, it's easy to lose track of the schedule!

HUH?

HA HA HA HA HA ?

My stars! You're back at last! You've been gone for days.

Fortunately, I have Gladys to take care of me!

I really appreciate correspondence courses. For some reason, the college wouldn't let her attend classes.

But, Granny, we left only a few hours ago!

Egad!

I can't figure out what day it is!

It's weird! Time seems to be passing at different rates in different places!

Oh my stars—time bubbles! This is bad, very bad indeed...

Will you tell me what's going on? You're starting to scare me...

Take a seat, child. I have a story to tell.

Tap

Plunk

First of all, let me make one thing clear: this valley is unlike any other place in the world!

For ages untold, a being of immense power has been imprisoned here. And yet, although he remains bound, his magic seeps out!

Whoa... who is this superpowered being?

That is a story for another time. As I was saying, a great enchantment was forged to confine this being's power, and four guardians were appointed— the sovereigns of the four seasons!

Since then, to fulfill their duty and protect the valley, the kings and queens of spring, summer, autumn, and winter wield in turn the Crown of Seasons!

The what?

The Crown of Seasons!

The Crown of Seasons isolates this being and controls his magic. The valley and its inhabitants remain safe only because we wield this power!

What do you mean by "we"? Are you...?

HEE HEE

Yes! I am the Queen of Summer!

But...how is that possible?

Long ago, the Queen of Summer was no different from the other sovereigns. She was wise, however, and when the first human settlers began establishing their homesteads here...

...she alone recognized the necessity of integrating humans into their great enterprise.

The only way to accomplish this goal, she knew, was to abdicate and pass on her powers to a human. She chose an enthusiastic young shepherd girl...me.

And so, for eight hundred years, I have reigned as Queen of Summer.

Betcha never guessed, huh?!

I'm well-preserved for my age!

Alas, the power of the crown is too strong for a human, so I stashed part of it in my shepherd's staff.

I don't have to worry about being consumed by magic, and it's a handy weapon.

My fellow sovereigns graciously accepted my elevation—all except the king of Autumn. He's a rather surly fellow—not terribly fond of humans. But there's never been a problem... until this year.

What happened?

You.

Me?!

Yes, you. I suspect that one of the wishes you made to the trickster Rapscallion has upset the apple cart, as it were.

When I died in the other reality, you must have become the new Queen of Summer!

OH!

It wouldn't be such a bother—only you brought my staff back into the new reality.

Now the power of the crown has become fragmented, divided among you, me, and our staffs. The strain is too great, and the valley is being overwhelmed by raw magic.

The first sign of trouble is the appearance of time bubbles—fractures in time itself. Unless we act quickly, even more dire consequences will follow.

Okay...so what's the plan?

The first step is to reunify the power of the crown. I need you to scurry back to your house as quickly as possible and retrieve your staff.

We have uncovered vital information! If the staff thingy has magic power, the boss will want it right away! It's our job to get it before the snot-nosed kid does!

...

YES, CHIEF!

CLAK

What's the next step?

Once we have both staffs, you abdicate in my favor, I pass the crown to the King of Autumn, and this whole unfortunate incident will be over.

Just like that?

Just like that.

Great, let's go! There's not a moment to lose!

Is it me, or did that puppy just speak Human?

Human, tell us what we want to know! We are the Chest—

The Chestnut Knights! I don't believe it!

Huh?

OMG! OMG! You're real! I heard tons of stories about you when I was growing up! You were my heroes! I'm your number-one fan! You are so cool!

Really? I had no idea we were famous...

Are you kidding?

Burr, the warrior who dreams of becoming a tree!

...

The mysterious Hull, whose every word is a gift!

And Leaf, their honorable and intrepid chief! You're real! It's all true!

Um...thanks. That's nice. Do you know where your daughter's staff is?

No idea. I can never keep track of where she keeps her stuff. Why?

SILENCE! WE'RE ASKING THE QUESTIONS!

SO WHAT NOW, CHIEF?

We take him to the boss.

After the fox gets done with him, he won't have any secrets left. Besides, we can use him as a hostage. Chestnut knights—forward!

The Chestnut knights have taken me hostage! So cool!

Am I seeing what I think I see—a bird frozen in flight?

We'd better hurry— matters are getting worse.

Terrible...

...isn't it?

Whoa!

You're the Queen of Summer's friend, aren't you? I've been keeping an eye on you.

Let there be no mistake. If I don't get the crown soon, everything will be reduced to dust.

I hope she's told you—this is only the beginning!

I...

All set—
let's go!

WHAT???

The other part of the crown is in the possession of that snot-nosed kid?!

Fools! If you hadn't dawdled, I'd have the crown already!

Well, boss, we did take her father hostage. That's something, isn't it?

We can't waste time on negotiation. Raw magic is about to tear the valley apart. Kill him! And then let's go get that staff.

Um...excuse me?

HEY, BOSS, THIS GUY AIN'T SO BAD! THERE'S NO NEED TO OFF HIM!

How dare you?

My brother is right—he's harmless. We should let him go.

Listen up, pip-squeaks! The humans have violated the agreement! They deserve no mercy!

He's a human! So cut his throat!

But, boss...

But nothing!

Snick

I'm rather fond of this human.

All right—bring him along. He can be your servant!

The Chestnut knights saved my life... Too cool!

What just happened?

We got caught in a bubble. They're everywhere! At least we're aware of the passage of time now.

I can't stand much more of this!

You can say that again! Come on—shake a leg. We've lost enough time!

What exactly are you doing here?

I am Leaf, Captain of the Chestnut knights, in the service of the Fox, king of Autumn.

Well, I'm Aster, Interim Co-Sovereign of Summer, and you're going to tell me what I want to know!

Where's my father? And Granny?

Lady Aster, we had planned to exchange your father for your staff and thus force the other Queen of Summer to give us her power.

But nothing went according to plan.

CLING

By the time we arrived, a time bubble had engulfed her cabin, greatly accelerating the passage of time.

Everything was in ruins; the only thing left was her staff, the twin of the one you now carry. I'm sorry—I fear your friend is dead.

Our boss was exceedingly upset, because without the crown, he thought it would be impossible for him to begin his reign.

Okay—I see.
Makes sense.

Really?

Of course not! Nothing makes sense! Why does he want to involve the Queen of Spring? Weren't things complicated enough already?!

I think he hopes to save us by wielding the power of another Sovereign of the Seasons! But all he'll do is destroy the balance of nature!

By killing spring, the fox can stop the time bubbles, but only by destroying the valley!

Okay, then we need to stop him. That much is clear. But why is he taking my father along?

If he fails, the fox will need your father to serve as a receptacle to recover the power of the Queen of Spring.

That's not so bad...

Of course, your father will die, but the fox is risking his own life in this process.

Holy cow! Well, don't just stand there! Where do we find the Queen of Spring?

Allow me to be your guide! Henceforth, I place myself at your service, my lady!

Well...okay. Sounds good!

This way!

Wow!

Yes! YES! I shall have all the power I need to save the valley...and my rule shall last forever!

Wait...what?! That's all?! It won't be enough!

ROOOAR

What do we do now, Aster?

Well...I've won, haven't I? I'm the Queen of Summer.

Alas, my lady, you are too inexperienced to wield such power. And the fox is in no condition...

POOF

Tell me, honey, do you have adventures like this every time you take a walk?

Not exactly, Dad. Some days are better than others. Today was... not bad.

Really? Uh...you still need to be careful!

Hello, Granny! How are you?

Well enough. Come over here, child. The King of Winter certainly hasn't wasted any time.

Oh, it's not so bad! At least we can have a calm discussion with him.

By the way, my father has finally found a job!

Really? What?

He is writing the chronicles of the Chestnut Knights!

Good for him. Now hold out your hands—I have a gift for you.

Oh!

Do you want me to take care of him?

I'm too old for such nonsense. He has to regain his full strength before next autumn.

He must also learn to appreciate humans.

Yawn

It's a big responsibility, but I have faith in you.

Now that I think about it, Granny, why are there no sheep here in the valley? Everywhere else, wool comes from sheep, not dogs.

My child, that is a long story, a long story indeed...

Aster and the Accidental Magic was thumbnailed with pen on paper, then inked and colored in Photoshop. The book is lettered in Hawthorn.

THE
CHARACTERS
OF ASTER

ASTER

BUZZ

Aster has a strong personality for a ten-year-old. As a city dweller, she is NOT enthusiastic about the idea of moving to the mountains. But she can't resist the call of adventure, and it looks like this nowhere town might have more than enough excitement for Aster and her new friends.

Buzz is a small woolly dog who doesn't have wool. He's Aster's closest and most loyal friend, and was given to her by Granny. It turns out that he's really chatty, as Aster quickly finds out once he gains the ability to talk.

MOM

DAD

Aster's mother is a well-known ornithologist (person who knows a lot about birds) who moved her family to the mountains so she could continue her studies and stop the invasion of giant destructive crows. She tends to analyze every situation with a scientific approach.

Aster's father has quit his job to follow his family to the middle of nowhere. Since he grew up in the mountains, he knows a little about the environment...and some of the characters Aster might come across. Too bad he can't help being bored to death anyway.

GRANNY

THE TRICKSTER RAPSCALLION

Who is that mysterious old shepherdess who keeps giving Aster weird advice? And why does she have woolly dogs instead of sheep?

One of the oldest and most powerful spirits of the universe...beware of the wishes he grants! He is good at twisting other people's words for his own amusement.

THE KING OF AUTUMN

THE KING OF WINTER

The king of Autumn is a fox who means business. Despite his good intentions for the countryside, his hatred of humans stops him from finding a peaceful solution.

The king of Winter is a mountain. He takes up a lot of space, but he is good-natured and has a great sense of humor. Nobody knows where he comes from, but it's clear that he's been around for a very long time.

THE
CHESTNUT
KNIGHTS

HULL

LEAF

BURR

The Chestnut knights are
legendary mountain warriors
who follow their hearts.
They might be in service
to the king of Autumn, but
that doesn't mean they can't
make up their own minds
about the situations they
find themselves in.

Aster

BUZZ AND *The* CHESTNUT **KNIGHTS**

will return in...

RH GRAPHIC
THE DEBUT LIST

BUG BOYS
By Laura Knetzger

Bugs, friends, the world around us—this book has everything! Come explore *Bug Boys* for the fun, thoughtful adventure of growing up and being yourself.

Chapter Book

THE RUNAWAY PRINCESS
By Johan Troïanowski

The castle is quiet.
And dull.
And boring.
Escape on a quest for excitement with our runaway princess, Robin!

Middle-Grade

ASTER AND THE ACCIDENTAL MAGIC
By Thom Pico & Karensac

Nothing fun ever happens in the middle of the country . . . except maybe . . . magic? That's just the beginning of absolutely everything going wrong for Aster.

Middle-Grade

WITCHLIGHT
By Jessi Zabarsky

Lelek doesn't have any friends or family in the world. And then she meets Sanja. Swords, magic, falling in love . . . these characters come together in a journey to heal the wounds of the past.

Young Adult

FIND US ONLINE AT @RHKIDSGRAPHIC AND RHKIDSGRAPHIC.COM